William Shakespeare

Romeo and Juliet

Retold by
Marcia Williams

WALKER
BOOKS

William Shakespeare

Romeo and Juliet

First published 2015 by Walker Books Ltd
87 Vauxhall Walk, London SE11 5HJ

2 4 6 8 10 9 7 5 3 1

© 1998, 2014, 2015 Marcia Williams

This book has been typeset in Kennerly Regular

Printed and bound in Germany

British Library Cataloguing in Publication Data:
a catalogue record for this book is available from the British Library

ISBN 978-1-4063-6276-3

www.walker.co.uk

Contents

In which Romeo loves Rosaline.

In the beautiful old Italian city of Verona,
Lord Capulet was planning a grand banquet.
All the noble families in the city were
invited – all except the Montague family.
The Capulets and Montagues were sworn
enemies. They had been feuding for as long
as anyone could remember, and their quarrel
ran so deep that even their servants fought.
If a member of the Capulet household passed

a member of the Montague household on the street, the peaceful city would suddenly erupt in violence. The Prince of Verona was no longer prepared to tolerate this situation. He had decreed that the next Capulet or Montague to disturb the peace would pay with his life.

Lord Capulet had invited all the fairest ladies of Verona to the banquet including his own niece, Rosaline. She had many suitors but, unknown to Lord Capulet, the most passionate of all was a young nobleman named Romeo, son of his enemy, Lord Montague! Romeo was a romantic young man. His infatuation with Rosaline caused him much heartache, for Rosaline was a faithful Montague and scorned Romeo.

Day and night, Romeo was either wandering the streets of Verona looking for Rosaline or boring his friends, Benvolio and Mercutio, with tales of her great beauty. So when they heard that she would be at Lord Capulet's party, they persuaded Romeo to go with them, disguised behind a mask. They hoped

to show him that there were many ladies in Verona who were even fairer than Rosaline. "Compare her face with some that I shall show, and I will make thee think thy swan a crow," said Benvolio.

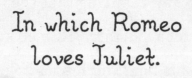

In which Romeo loves Juliet.

Old Lord Capulet was in a jovial mood on the evening of his party. "Welcome gentlemen! Ladies that have their toes unplagued with corns will have a bout with you. Come musicians, play!" he said.

He encouraged all the young folk to enjoy the dancing, including his daughter, Juliet, who soon took to the floor with a dashing knight. She was so merry and so very pretty

that even the love-struck Romeo noticed
her. Indeed, not realizing that she was
Lord Capulet's daughter, Romeo suddenly
found that his heart no longer belonged
to Rosaline, but to Juliet! "O, she doth
teach the torches to burn bright! Did my
heart love till now?" he breathed.

Romeo did not keep his feelings to
himself but, as if in a dream, stood
declaring his new love to all about him.

Unfortunately, Lord Capulet's fiery nephew, Tybalt, recognized his voice. "This, by his voice, should be a Montague," he angrily cried. "To strike him dead I hold it not a sin!"

Tybalt called for his sword and had it not been for Lord Capulet, who forbade fighting at his ball, the evening would certainly have ended in bloodshed. Lord Capulet insisted that Tybalt make Romeo welcome. Tybalt

unwillingly sheathed his sword, but he
swore he would take revenge on Romeo at
some other time.

Romeo was quite unaware of this passing
danger. He waited until Juliet stopped
dancing and then began to woo her. Juliet
was entranced by Romeo and even allowed
him to steal a kiss. Their few minutes
together seemed to them like hours.

When Juliet was called away by her

mother, Romeo realized she was a Capulet, but he didn't care. And when Juliet's nurse told her that Romeo was a Montague, her heart was too full of love to take notice of a family feud. "My only love sprung from my only hate!" she cried.

As the party ended, Romeo and his friends set off to make merry elsewhere, but Benvolio and Mercutio soon found themselves walking along the road on their own.

Romeo, as if pulled by a thread, had turned back to Juliet's house. He climbed over the high orchard wall and stood hidden in the shadows, searching the house for signs of life. He knew he was risking death by being there, and his heart pounded. Then a light appeared at one of the windows and Juliet stepped onto the balcony.

"O, it is my love!" whispered Romeo. He hid behind a tree and listened as Juliet declared her love for him to the stars!

"O Romeo. 'Tis but thy name that is my enemy. Thou art thyself though, not a Montague," she said.

To Romeo, Juliet looked more beautiful than the sun itself, and encouraged by her loving words, he revealed himself. Both knew the danger he was in, but they could not think of parting. They fell so deeply in love that they agreed to wed the following day – in secret, in case their feuding families tried to part them. In the heat of this new passion, Juliet quite forgot that she was betrothed to Paris, a noble of her father's choice.

Dawn was breaking when Juliet's nurse finally persuaded her back into her room. "Good night, good night! Parting is such sweet sorrow that I shall say good night till it be morrow!" cried Juliet as she ran inside.

Romeo raced straight to the monastery where his good friend Friar Laurence lived. The friar asked Romeo if he had some good news from Rosaline.

"Rosaline? I have forgot that name!" cried Romeo joyously.

The friar was surprised to hear this, and even more surprised that Romeo had so quickly found a new love, for he had heard so much of Rosaline over the past weeks.

However, Friar Laurence believed that Romeo's heart was true, so he agreed to marry Romeo to his Juliet. The friar was a friend to both the Montagues and the Capulets and hoped that the marriage would unite the families and end the years of feuding.

That very afternoon, Juliet joined Romeo at the chapel of the monastery and the happy sweethearts were wed.

Afterwards they parted, as they knew
they must, until Friar Laurence had broken
the news to their families. Both were
impatient for the coming night when Romeo
planned to climb the wall into the Capulets'
orchard one last time, so that he could spend
some stolen moments with his new bride.

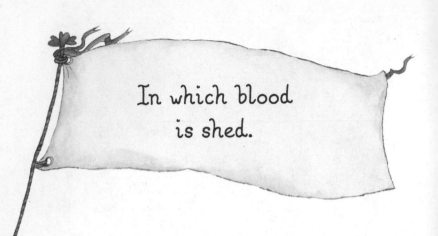

In which blood
is shed.

When Romeo returned from his wedding at the chapel the streets of Verona were deserted, for it was the time of day when all people of sense rested in the cool of their homes. So Romeo was surprised to run into his friends Benvolio and Mercutio, who were arguing with Tybalt.

"Mercutio, thou consort'st with Romeo," cried Tybalt, spoiling for a fight.

The last thing on Romeo's mind was

fighting; all his thoughts were consumed by
love. Besides, he was now related to Tybalt
by marriage, and the name Capulet had
suddenly become very dear to him. So Romeo
did his best to calm Tybalt. But Tybalt was
determined to take revenge on Romeo for
gatecrashing Lord Capulet's party.

When Romeo refused to fight, Mercutio
stepped in to fight in his place, even though
Romeo tried to stop him. "Tybalt, Mercutio,
the prince expressly hath forbidden
bandying in Verona streets!" Romeo cried.

His words had no effect. Tybalt and
Mercutio clashed swords, and as Romeo

stepped in to part them, Tybalt's sword
plunged into Mercutio's chest.

"A plague o' both your houses! They have made worms' meat of me," cried Mercutio. The wound was fatal and soon poor Mercutio lay dead in Romeo's arms.

Mercutio's death sent Romeo into a sudden rage. He grabbed a rapier and lunged at Tybalt, and before Romeo even realized what he was doing, Tybalt also lay dead.

As Romeo looked at Tybalt's lifeless body, his anger left him. But it was too late – he had killed his wife's cousin. "O! I am fortune's fool," he cried. Romeo knew that the Prince of Verona might condemn him to death if he was arrested, so he fled to the sanctuary of Friar Laurence's cell.

In which a hatched plan begins to go awry.

When the Prince of Verona heard that
Romeo had been provoked, he did not
condemn him to death. However, his
patience with the feuding families was
at an end, so he banished
Romeo from Verona.

Oh, unhappy Juliet! At first she was furious with Romeo and wept copious tears for her dead cousin. "O God! Did Romeo's hand shed Tybalt's blood? O serpent heart, hid with a flowering face!"

Then her thoughts turned to her new husband. "My husband lives, that Tybalt would have slain!" Her love for Romeo changed her tears of sorrow to tears of joy.

Romeo came to see Juliet that night. He quickly secured her forgiveness and held her in his arms. Yet the night was tinged with sadness, not only because of the adventures of the day, but also because the lovers knew that they had to part and had no way of knowing when they would be together again.

The morning dawned far too soon for them. Juliet tried to persuade Romeo that the morning song of the larks was the nightly call of the nightingale. But the sky was streaked with morning light and they had to say farewell. As Romeo set out for

Mantua, where he would be safe from arrest, he promised to take every opportunity to send Juliet his greetings. They both prayed that Friar Laurence would soon secure a pardon for Romeo and pacify their families.

When Romeo left Juliet, he promised that they would soon be reunited and all their troubles would be forgotten. Poor Romeo – if he had known of Lord Capulet's plan, he might not have been so sure. For before Friar Laurence had a chance to share the news of Romeo and Juliet's marriage, Lord Capulet told Juliet's suitor, Paris, that he could marry Juliet in a few days' time. He hoped that a wedding would cheer his daughter after her cousin's death.

In vain, Juliet pleaded with her father not

 to rush her into marriage. She pointed out that she was only thirteen years old, too young to get married! She reminded him that Tybalt had only just died, and said she was too distressed to find any joy in such a union. But Paris was a rich, noble suitor and her father was determined. No daughter in Verona could refuse her father, and Juliet did not dare reveal the

true obstacle to the wedding: her marriage to Romeo.

With Romeo already on his way to

Mantua, Juliet did not know what to do, so she ran to Friar Laurence to seek his advice.

In desperation they agreed a devious and dangerous plot.

 Juliet went home and, to her father's joy, agreed to marry Paris. The whole

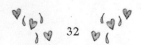

household began to bustle with
preparations for this sudden wedding.
Guests were invited, flowers arranged,
furniture polished and gowns stitched.
Then, just before Juliet was due to put on

her wedding dress, she took a drug which
would make her appear dead for forty-two
hours.

When Juliet's nurse went to wake her, she thought at first that Juliet was in a deep sleep. "Why, lamb! Why, lady! Fie, you slug-a-bed!" she said. She tried to tease Juliet awake, then shake her awake, but the poor woman soon realized it was hopeless.

Juliet's family were devastated – they were convinced that Juliet was dead. The wedding party became a funeral procession.

Juliet was carried to the family burial vault, from where, according to the friar's plan, Romeo would soon rescue her.

Unfortunately, a messenger reached
Romeo with the false news of Juliet's
"death" before the friar's letter, which would
have told him that she was only drugged.

Poor Romeo, knowing nothing of the friar's
plan, was thrown into the deepest despair.
"Is it even so?" he cried in anguish. Only a
moment earlier he had been so full of joy
and expectation, believing he would be
reunited with Juliet, imagining their future

happiness. Now he believed that both she and his dreams were dead.

Romeo called for a horse to be saddled while he went to a local apothecary to buy poison – he had decided to return to Verona and die beside his sweetheart. "Well, Juliet, I will lie with thee tonight!" he cried, as he set off to see her for the last time.

In which the tragedy is complete.

It was midnight when Romeo arrived at the graveyard where the Capulets' tomb lay. The mourners were long departed and only the yew trees stood sentinel beside the tomb. Then out of the darkness came the weeping figure of Paris. He had come to throw flowers on Juliet's grave on what would have been their wedding night. Paris recognized Romeo at once. He knew he was a Montague and he thought that he must have come to cause mischief at his enemies' tomb.

Romeo was not looking for a fight and longed to be left alone to die at Juliet's side. When Paris tried to apprehend him, Romeo tried to shake him off, but Paris was like an angry jackal and would not set him free. And so they fought. Romeo stabbed Paris, who fell backwards upon the rough ground.

"O, I am slain! If thou be merciful, open the tomb, lay me with Juliet," Paris begged.

"In faith, I will," cried the unhappy Romeo.

Romeo opened the tomb and gazed upon Juliet with so much love and sorrow that he hardly needed poison to stop his breaking heart. He lifted Paris in his arms and lay him beside her. Then he gazed upon his true love's face.

"Death, that hath sucked the honey of thy breath, hath had no power yet upon thy

beauty," he said. He gave her one last kiss. "Here's to my love!" he said, drinking the poison. "O true apothecary! Thy drugs are quick. Thus with a kiss I die."

At that moment, Friar Laurence arrived at the graveyard, spade, lantern and crowbar in hand. He had only recently discovered that his letter had not reached Romeo, and his first thought was to rush and save Juliet from her tomb. Then he planned to find Romeo and tell him the joyous news that his love was still alive. As his old feet stumbled through the graves, he thought he saw a lantern flicker by the Capulets' tomb. Could it be Romeo? Had he arrived too late? "O, much I fear some ill unlucky thing," he muttered.

He entered the tomb and saw both Paris and Romeo dead beside the sleeping Juliet.

"Romeo! Alack, alack!" the friar cried out, disturbing Juliet's unnatural sleep.

"O, comfortable friar, where is my lord?" she asked as she awoke.

"Thy husband in thy bosom there lies dead; and Paris too," said Friar Laurence.

Hearing the night watch approach, Friar Laurence urged Juliet to flee with him

before they were blamed for the death of
both young men. But Juliet would not leave
Romeo. She kissed his lips, hoping to find
some poison there, but there was none.

Quickly, before the watch could stop
her, Juliet picked up Romeo's dagger and
stabbed herself. "O happy dagger. This
is thy sheath; there rust and let me die!"
she cried. Then she fell upon her beloved
Romeo's body and died.

When the Montagues and Capulets
arrived upon this tragic scene, they were
grief-stricken. The friar was summoned
by the Prince of Verona and he related the
whole story; how Romeo and Juliet had
fallen in love; how he had married the pair
hoping that their union would end their
families' bitter feud; how his letter to Romeo
had been delayed. The Prince of Verona
rebuked Lord Capulet and Lord Montague

for their feud, as it was this and not the
friar's plan which was the true cause of this
tragedy. "Never was a story of more woe
than this of Juliet and her Romeo," he said.

The two old enemies were overcome with
sorrow and guilt.

"Poor sacrifices of our enmity," wept Lord
Montague.

"O brother Montague," cried Lord
Capulet, "give me your hand."

The grieving fathers each vowed to raise a golden statue to the other's child. Thus they buried their feud along with their precious children, Romeo and his sweet Juliet.

WILLIAM SHAKESPEARE was a popular playwright, poet and actor who lived in Elizabethan England. He married in Stratford-upon-Avon aged eighteen and had three children, although one died in childhood. Shakespeare then moved to London, where he wrote 39 plays and over 150 sonnets, many of which are still very popular today. In fact, his plays are performed more often than those of any other playwright, and he died 450 years ago! His gravestone includes a curse against interfering with his burial place, possibly to deter people from opening it in search of unpublished manuscripts. It reads, "Blessed be the man that spares these stones, and cursed be he that moves my bones." Spooky!

MARCIA WILLIAMS' mother was a novelist and her father a playwright, so it's not surprising that Marcia ended up an author herself. Although she never trained formally as an artist, she found that motherhood, and the time she spent later as a nursery school teacher, inspired her to start writing and illustrating children's books.

Marcia's books bring to life some of the world's all-time favourite stories and some colourful historical characters. Her hilarious retellings and clever observations will have children laughing out loud and coming back for more!

More retellings from Marcia Williams

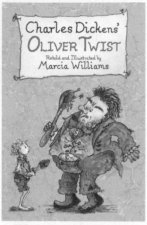

ISBN 978-1-4063-5692-2

ISBN 978-1-4063-5693-9

ISBN 978-1-4063-5694-6

ISBN 978-1-4063-5695-3

Available from all good booksellers

www.walker.co.uk